WARRIORS

RAVENPAW'S PATH

#3: THE HEART OF A WARRIOR

Jolley, Dan.
Warriors. Ravenpaw's
path. #3, The heart of a
c2010.
33305237736776
mi   04/14/17

WARRIORS

RAVENPAW'S PATH

#3: THE HEART OF A WARRIOR

CREATED BY
ERIN HUNTER

WRITTEN BY
DAN JOLLEY

ART BY
JAMES L. BARRY

HAMBURG // LONDON // LOS ANGELES // TOKYO

HARPER
An Imprint of HarperCollinsPublishers

Warriors: Ravenpaw's Path Vol. 3: The Heart of a Warrior
Created by Erin Hunter
Written by Dan Jolley
Art by James L. Barry

Digital Tones - Lincy Chan
Lettering - John Hunt
Cover Design - Louis Csontos

Editor - Lillian Diaz-Przybyl
Managing Editor - Vy Nguyen
Print-Production Manager - Lucas Rivera
Art Director - Al-Insan Lashley
Director of Sales and Manufacturing - Allyson DeSimone
Associate Publisher - Marco Pavia
President and C.O.O. - John Parker
C.E.O. and Chief Creative Officer - Stu Levy

A  Manga

TOKYOPOP and are trademarks or registered trademarks of TOKYOPOP Inc.

TOKYOPOP Inc.
5900 Wilshire Blvd. Suite 2000
Los Angeles, CA 90036

E-mail: info@TOKYOPOP.com
Come visit us online at www.TOKYOPOP.com

Text copyright © 2010 by Working Partners Limited
Art copyright © 2010 by TOKYOPOP Inc. and HarperCollins Publishers
All rights reserved. Printed in the United States of America.
No part of this book may be used or reproduced in any manner whatsoever without written permission
except in the case of brief quotations embodied in critical articles and reviews. This manga is a work of
fiction. Any resemblance to actual events or locales or persons, living or dead, is entirely coincidental.
For information address HarperCollins Children's Books, a division of HarperCollins Publishers,
195 Broadway, New York, NY 10007
www.harpercollinschildrens.com

ISBN 978-0-06-168867-6
Library of Congress catalog card number: 2010921890

16   PC/BV   10 9 8
❖
First Edition

Hello!

Welcome to the final part of Ravenpaw's trilogy. All of you who wished he had stayed in ThunderClan and become a warrior, are you proud that he fought so well in Book Two on behalf of his former Clanmates? He never forgot his battle training, or what it meant to be loyal to a Clan. You can understand why Barley was afraid that Ravenpaw might want to stay in the forest now that Tigerstar has gone.

But Ravenpaw knows himself better than that. If home is where the heart is, his heart is firmly rooted in the barn with his best friend. Ravenpaw will have to call on the combat skills he learned long ago to drive out the cats who took over the farm, but deep down Ravenpaw knows he is not a warrior. He is loyal and brave and quick-thinking, but his path lies in a different direction than the Clans'.

So now do you see why Ravenpaw was never destined to have a warrior name? His name will be Ravenpaw forever, and he wears it with pride. Ravenpaw represents everything that is good about choosing your own path and having the courage to stick to it—but without forgetting any of the lessons learned along the way.

Best wishes always,
Erin Hunter

IT'S HARD TO BELIEVE I'M HERE.

BACK IN THE THUNDERCLAN CAMP.

CATS YAWN AND STRETCH ALL AROUND ME AS THEY WAKE UP...

...AND INSTEAD OF DOGS BARKING OR ROOSTERS CROWING, ALL I HEAR IS THE SONG OF BIRDS IN THE FOREST.

MY NAME IS RAVENPAW. MY BEST FRIEND, BARLEY, AND I WERE FORCED OUT OF OUR HOME ON THE FARM BY A GROUP OF ROGUES...

...AND WE CAME TO THUNDERCLAN FOR HELP.

WHAT BROUGHT US HERE WAS PRETTY HORRIBLE...BUT I REALLY DO ENJOY BEING HERE.

I WAS BORN INTO THUNDERCLAN, AFTER ALL.

WATCHING THE HUNTING PATROLS HEADING OUT...

...SEEING THE CLAN CATS TOGETHER, YOUNG AND OLD...

IT'S TAKEN ME LESS TIME THAN I EXPECTED TO GET USED TO ALL THIS AGAIN.

IT'S HARD TO BELIEVE ONLY THREE DAYS HAVE PASSED SINCE BARLEY AND I HELPED THUNDERCLAN DEFEAT SOME OTHER ROGUES...

...A BUNCH OF SCAVENGERS FROM TWOLEGPLACE.

THOSE MANGY CATS WON'T BE AMBUSHING ANY MORE CLAN HUNTING PATROLS NOW.

AND TODAY, FIRESTAR'S MAKING GOOD ON HIS PROMISE.

HE'S GOING TO HELP BARLEY AND ME RECLAIM OUR FARM.

TODAY, BARLEY AND I ARE GOING HOME!

THERE'S FIRESTAR NOW.

WE OWE HIM SO MUCH FOR AGREEING TO HELP US TAKE BACK THE FARM.

READY?

YES!

IT'S TIME!

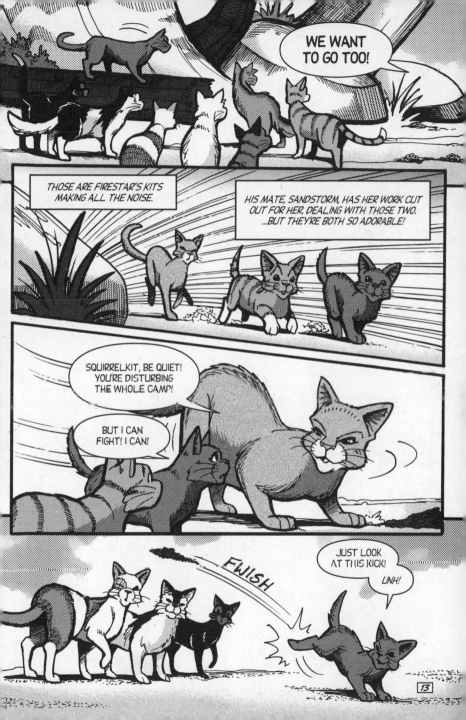

SANDSTORM'S WARNING COMES TOO LATE. SQUIRRELKIT'S RUCKUS WAKES EVERYONE UP.

THEY COME TO SEE WHAT SQUIRRELKIT'S MAKING ALL THE NOISE ABOUT...

...AND HERE WE ARE. RIGHT OUT IN THE OPEN. OBVIOUSLY ABOUT TO LEAVE.

BARLEY'S HANDLING ALL THE ATTENTION A LITTLE BETTER THAN I THOUGHT HE WOULD, ACTUALLY.

ALL RIGHT, EVERYONE. LET US THROUGH.

IT'S TIME TO GO.

THUNDERCLAN'S GOOD-BYES AND THANK-YOUS RING IN MY EARS AS WE TRAVEL.

PART OF ME WANTS TO STAY... BUT ONLY A SMALL PART.

FORMER THUNDERCLAN CAT OR NOT, I BELONG ON THE FARM.

RUNNING THROUGH THE FOREST, THOUGH, AS PART OF A WARRIOR PATROL...THAT'S HARD TO BEAT.

WARRIORS--HOLD UP. BE READY.

NO, GRAYSTRIPE... THERE'S NO NEED.

OUR FRIENDS FROM WINDCLAN ARE EXPECTING US.

DEADFOOT. GOOD TO SEE YOU.

AND YOU, FIRESTAR.

RAVENPAW...BARLEY. WE'VE HEARD ABOUT WHAT HAPPENED AT THE FARM.

GOOD LUCK TO YOU BOTH. YOU DESERVE TO GET YOUR HOME BACK.

THANK YOU...THAT MEANS A LOT!

LOOKS LIKE WE HAVE FRIENDS IN MORE THAN ONE CLAN NOW...!

CLOUDTAIL--TAKE A HUNTING PATROL OUT, BUT KEEP YOUR DISTANCE FROM THE FARM.

SURE THING.

THE REST OF YOU, STICK WITH RAVENPAW AND ME.

RAVENPAW, I'D LIKE TO SCOUT THE FARMYARD. WOULD YOU SHOW US THE WAY?

OF COURSE.

WE KEEP OUR NOSES TO THE WIND, ALERT FOR THE ROGUES' SCENT.

WE CAN'T LET THEM KNOW WE'RE HERE.

NOT YET.

IT BREAKS MY HEART, WHAT GREETS US INSIDE THE BARN. THIS PLACE USED TO BE OUR HOME.

NOW IT'S A WRECK...AND IT STINKS OF STALE BEDDING AND CAT DIRT.

WE HEAR SOMEONE SNORING. SLEEPING, INSTEAD OF TAKING CARE OF WHERE THEY LIVE.

NOT ONLY THAT...BUT THOSE KITS ARE PLAYING WITH THEIR PREY. I DON'T THINK THEY'RE EVEN GOING TO EAT IT.

HOW WASTEFUL. HOW WRONG.

THE WARRIOR CODE FORBIDS WASTING FOOD LIKE THIS. I'M NO WARRIOR-- I DON'T HAVE TO LIVE BY THE CODE...

...BUT THIS MAKES ME SO ANGRY, I BARELY HEAR FIRESTAR CALLING FOR US TO LEAVE, THE BLOOD'S RUSHING SO LOUD IN MY EARS.

THE CHICKENS DON'T LIKE THE ROGUES...WILLIE AND HIS CREW KILLED SOME OF THEIR CHICKS RIGHT BEFORE WE LEFT.

BUT THEY ALWAYS LIKED RAVENPAW AND ME. THEY SHOULDN'T BE ANY TROUBLE.

ALL RIGHT. WE'LL WAIT FOR THE ROGUES TO SETTLE DOWN FOR THE NIGHT.

THEN WE'LL GO UNDER THE DOOR AGAIN AND AMBUSH THEM AS THEY SLEEP.

UNTIL THEN WE MUST STAY HIDDEN.

DO NOT LEAVE THIS SHED.

THAT'S NO TROUBLE. OUR PATROL BROUGHT BACK PLENTY OF FRESH-KILL. WE CAN STAY HERE JUST FINE.

IT'S TENSE, ALL THE WAITING.

SEVERAL OF THE OTHER CATS GET SOME SLEEP, BUT I CAN'T.

POOR BARLEY. HE'S LOOKING... OLDER. THIS WAS HIS HOME BEFORE IT WAS MINE.

THIS MUST BE SO HARD ON HIM.

VIOLET...

RAVENPAW. YOU OKAY?

YEAH, I'M FINE. JUST A LITTLE NERVOUS.

I OWE THIS TO BARLEY. I NEED TO MAKE HIS HOME SAFE AGAIN. HE WAS SO GENEROUS TO ME WHEN I NEEDED HELP.

DON'T WORRY, OLD FRIEND. WE'LL MAKE THIS RIGHT.

EXCEPT FOR THE DISTANT HOOT OF AN OWL, THE FARM IS SILENT AND STILL.

29

IT SEEMS LIKE THE PLAN'S GOING TO GO OFF WITHOUT A HITCH...

...UNTIL THE CHICKENS GIVE US A NASTY SURPRISE.

BUK KWAAWK!

BUK KWAAWK!

BUK KWAAWK!

WHAT'S GOING ON?

I DON'T KNOW! THEY NEVER USED TO BE THIS NERVOUS!

IT'S SNAPPER! HE MUST TAUNT THEM ALL THE TIME!

NOW THEY'RE SCARED OF ALL CATS!

32

WHAT THE...

GET OUT! SCOOT!

WHAM

ALL OF YOU, GET OUT!

I GET A GOOD, SOLID LOOK FOR THE FIRST TIME, AND IT CONFIRMS MY WORST FEAR.

THESE CATS ARE BLOODCLAN.

THEY'VE FOLLOWED US!

THERE ARE TOO MANY OF THEM!

THUNDERCLAN-- SCATTER! YOU KNOW WHERE TO MEET UP!

I CAN'T BELIEVE IT. IT'S LIKE A NIGHTMARE.

...I KNOW IT'S A LOT WORSE FOR BARLEY.

MY BROTHERS ARE HERE! I CAN'T GET AWAY FROM THEM... NO MATTER WHERE I GO, THEY WON'T LEAVE ME ALONE!

AND THEY'VE BROUGHT BLOODCLAN CATS TO OUR FARM!

BUT AS BAD AS IT IS FOR ME...

I'VE GOT TO DO SOMETHING.

NOW...LISTEN...THIS IS TERRIBLE, I'M NOT SAYING IT'S NOT. BUT IT MIGHT NOT BE AS BAD AS WE THINK.

THEY MIGHT NOT THINK OF THEMSELVES AS BLOODCLAN ANYMORE...AND IF SO, THAT MEANS THEY'RE VULNERABLE.

THOSE CATS WERE CALLING YOUR BROTHERS "JUMPER" AND "HOOT," NOT THEIR BLOODCLAN NAMES.

THE CLOUDS HANG LOW AND HEAVY THE NEXT DAY. I KEEP WAITING FOR IT TO RAIN, BUT IT NEVER DOES.

NO ONE'S LEFT THE BARN SINCE SUNUP.

WE USE THE TIME TO COME UP WITH A NEW PLAN OF ATTACK...

...AND I TRY NOT TO LET MY NERVES GET THE BEST OF ME.

FROM HERE THE PLACE LOOKS DESERTED.

THE BLOODCLAN CATS CHANGE EVERYTHING.

IS THERE ANY OTHER WAY INTO THE BARN BESIDES UNDER THE DOOR?

WELL....YES. YES, THERE IS!

THERE ARE HOLES IN THE ROOF, LEADING ONTO THE RAFTERS!

JUST THEN WE ALL NOTICE SOMETHING INTERESTING:

SNAPPER AND POUNCE TAKE OFF AS IF THEY ARE BEING CHASED BY FOXES.

COME ON! LET'S GET 'EM!

NO. STAY.

THEY KNOW THE TERRAIN. WITH THAT BIG OF A HEAD START, WE'D NEVER CATCH THEM.

WELL...GOOD RIDDANCE, I SAY.

THIS JUST SHOWS HOW SCARED THEY ARE--THEY CAN'T EVEN KEEP THEIR OWN FROM DESERTING.

...WE'LL SEE.

39

FINALLY WE COME UP WITH A PLAN. I THINK IT'S A GOOD ONE... IF NOTHING MESSES IT UP.

EVERYONE, LISTEN TO ME.

IT'S GOING TO HAPPEN LIKE THIS...

FIRESTAR EXPLAINS HIS PLAN QUICKLY AND CLEARLY. WE'LL BE ATTACKING ON TWO FRONTS.

SINCE THE DOOR WILL BE GUARDED, WE'LL SEND TWO CATS TO THE FRONT DOOR...

...THEN WE'LL SLIP DOWN THROUGH THE ROOF AND CATCH THEM BY SURPRISE.

THIS WILL WORK.

WE *WILL* DRIVE THEM OUT THIS TIME.

BAWK BAWK BUK KAAWK!

KAAWK!

FLIP

BAHK BUK-BUK KAAWK!

BUK KAAWWK!

GRAAHR BARK BARK BARK

THE CLAN CATS ARE BACK! GET THEM!

WHERE ARE THEY? ALL I SEE IS CHICKENS!

43

NOW--SHOW US A WAY IN!

THE CHICKENS ARE A PERFECT DISTRACTION! I SHOULD'VE KNOWN BETTER THAN TO QUESTION FIRESTAR.

RIGHT! THERE ARE GAPS IN THE ROOF, RIGHT OVER...

OH NO...

IT'S A HORRIBLE FEELING, THOUGH, WHEN I REALIZE I'M MESSING UP THE PLAN MYSELF.

THE ROOF'S BEEN MENDED SINCE THE FIRE!

THE HOLE WE USED TO CLIMB THROUGH--IT'S NOT HERE ANYMORE!

WHAT DO WE DO?

EVERYONE'S COUNTING ON US!

WE MAKE A HOLE.

TEAR

CRACK

POP

SO MANY OF THE ROGUES HAVE ALREADY RUN AWAY...

WE'RE LEFT WITH ONLY A FEW OF THEM.

BUT THERE'S ONE THAT I'M GLAD TO SEE. ONE I HAVE PERSONAL BUSINESS WITH.

GO, WILLIE. GET OUT OF HERE.

THIS IS NOT YOUR HOME.

WARRIORS! RETREAT AND REGROUP!

I STILL HAVE FAITH IN FIRESTAR. I KNOW IF HE CAN GET US TO SAFETY, WE CAN FIGURE OUT A WAY TO DEAL WITH THIS.

BUT GETTING US TO SAFETY...

...ALL OF A SUDDEN...

...ISN'T LOOKING TOO LIKELY.

I DON'T EVEN HAVE THE WORDS TO DESCRIBE THE FURY THE DOGS UNLEASH ON THE ROGUES.

AS FIERCE AND VICIOUS AS THE ROGUES ARE, THE DOGS ARE SO MUCH MORE TERRIBLE...

...IT'S LIKE WATCHING A FOREST FIRE.

RUN! WE'VE GOT TO RUN!

WHAT?

NO--NO, WAIT!

55

HELP US, BARLEY!

GRRRR...

WE DIDN'T KNOW THIS WAS YOUR PLACE, HONEST!

WILLIE TOLD US IT WAS *HIS* PLACE!

WE WOULDN'T HAVE COME HERE IF WE'D KNOWN IT WAS YOURS, BROTHER!

LIARS!

?

YOU KNEW FULL WELL, COWARDS!

I'M SORRY, MY FRIEND.

BUT I CAN'T LET YOU HURT THESE CATS.

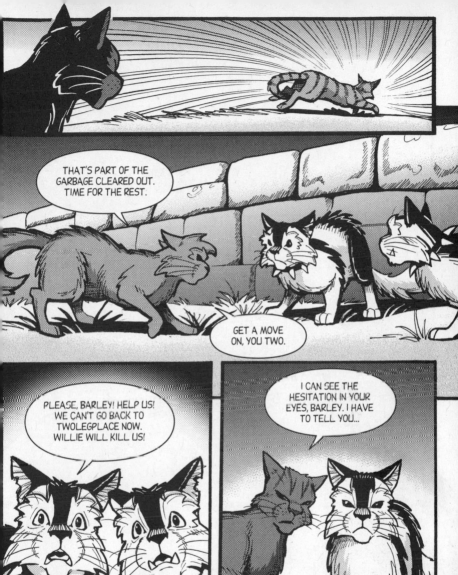

THAT'S PART OF THE GARBAGE CLEARED OUT. TIME FOR THE REST.

GET A MOVE ON, YOU TWO.

PLEASE, BARLEY! HELP US! WE CAN'T GO BACK TO TWOLEGPLACE NOW. WILLIE WILL KILL US!

COME ON, BARLEY...BROTHER.

I CAN SEE THE HESITATION IN YOUR EYES, BARLEY. I HAVE TO TELL YOU...

...LETTING THESE TWO TAKE ADVANTAGE OF YOUR GOOD NATURE WOULD BE UNWISE.

I CAN SEE THE CONFLICT IN BARLEY AS CLEARLY AS I CAN SEE THE STARS IN THE SKY.

HE CAN'T JUST SEND THESE ROGUES TO THEIR DEATHS.

LIKE IT OR NOT, THEY ARE FAMILY.

IT'S ALL RIGHT, FIRESTAR. IF BARLEY WANTS THEM TO STAY...

...I'LL MAKE SURE THERE AREN'T ANY PROBLEMS.

WELL...IF YOU'RE BOTH SURE...

I CAN ONLY IMAGINE WHAT THIS MUST BE LIKE FOR BARLEY.

LOSING HIS HOME...

DEALING WITH HIS BROTHERS...

HE LOOKS FRAILER THAN EVER.

IS THIS EVEN THE SAME PLACE, RAVENPAW?

I...I BARELY RECOGNIZE IT.

DON'T WORRY, BARLEY. WE'LL MAKE IT RIGHT AGAIN.

JUST LIKE OLD TIMES.

THANKS.

I GUESS THEY'RE READY TO GO BACK TO THEIR CAMP.

YEAH. WE'D BETTER SAY GOOD-BYE.

THANK YOU, FIRESTAR.

EVERYONE, THANK YOU. YOU RISKED YOUR LIVES FOR US.

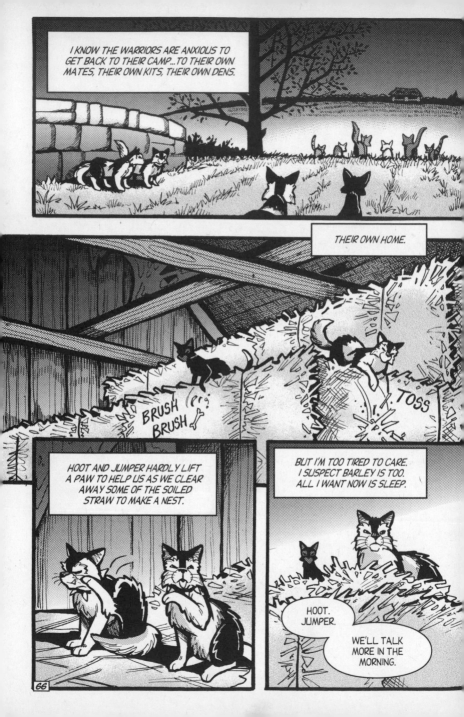

I KNOW THE WARRIORS ARE ANXIOUS TO GET BACK TO THEIR CAMP...TO THEIR OWN MATES, THEIR OWN KITS, THEIR OWN DENS.

THEIR OWN HOME.

BRUSH BRUSH

TOSS

HOOT AND JUMPER HARDLY LIFT A PAW TO HELP US AS WE CLEAR AWAY SOME OF THE SOILED STRAW TO MAKE A NEST.

BUT I'M TOO TIRED TO CARE. I SUSPECT BARLEY IS TOO. ALL I WANT NOW IS SLEEP.

HOOT. JUMPER.

WE'LL TALK MORE IN THE MORNING.

66

AS I WAKE UP, THE SOUNDS COME BACK TO ME.

THE COWS AND CHICKENS... THE TWOLEGS...THE CREAK OF THE BARN'S WOODEN WALLS...

WELL, ALMOST EVERYTHING. HOOT AND JUMPER ARE HERE NOW. WE'RE BACK...

I'M HOME AGAIN! I'M HOME, AND BARLEY IS HERE WITH ME, AND EVERYTHING IS RIGHT IN THE WORLD.

...BUT I WONDER...CAN THINGS EVER BE THE SAME AGAIN?

AS SOON AS I'M OUT OF SIGHT-- JUST GOING TO CATCH A MOUSE FOR BREAKFAST--I HEAR THEM TALKING TO BARLEY.

REMEMBER, BARLEY? REMEMBER ALL THE FUN WE USED TO HAVE PLAYING WHEN WE WERE ALL KITS?

AFTER THAT, I'M DONE. IT'S BEEN A LONG, HARD DAY, AFTER A WHOLE LOT OF LONG, HARD DAYS, AND I AM EXHAUSTED.

I'M BEAT. I'M GOING TO TAKE A NAP.

IF BARLEY COMES BACK BEFORE I WAKE UP, JUST TELL HIM WHERE I AM, OKAY?

I CAN...BARELY KEEP MY EYES OPEN...

I HAVE NO IDEA HOW LONG I'VE BEEN ASLEEP.

BUT I CAN TELL IMMEDIATELY THAT IT'S BARLEY SHAKING ME AWAKE.

WHAT? WHAT? WHAT'S WRONG?

TAKE A LOOK AROUND! YOU TELL ME WHAT'S WRONG!

WH...WHAT?

HOOT! JUMPER!

WHAT DID YOU DO? WHY HAVE YOU WRECKED THE PLACE LIKE THIS?

WE WERE ONLY TRYING TO CATCH MICE, RAVENPAW. IT'S DIFFICULT!

YEAH!

WE REALLY NEED SOMEONE TO SHOW US HOW, YOU KNOW.

WHAT'RE YOU TALKING AB—

BARLEY, I DID SHOW THEM! I SPENT ALL DAY SHOWING THEM!

I CAN'T HEAR WHAT HOOT WHISPERS IN BARLEY'S EAR.

BUT I DON'T HAVE TO KNOW THE WORDS TO GET THE GIST OF IT.

BARLEY?

BARLEY. WHAT'S GOING ON?

HOOT SAYS YOU GOT HIM AND JUMPER TO COLLECT ALL THE HERBS AND SUPPLIES WHILE YOU TOOK A NAP.

TH-THAT'S NOT TRUE!

THEY'RE LYING!

LOOK, I CAN TELL YOU'RE EXHAUSTED. I'M SURE YOU DON'T WANT ANY TROUBLE. I KNOW I DON'T.

YOU JUST WANT TO REST, RIGHT?

I CAN'T BELIEVE BARLEY WOULD BELIEVE THEM OVER ME, EVEN FOR A HEARTBEAT!

IT FLUSTERS ME SO BADLY, I CAN'T EVEN SAY ANYTHING. BUT I DO KNOW THIS:

I AM *SICK* OF THOSE TWO.

YOU KNOW, BARLEY...

THIS PLACE IS MUCH NICER, NOW THAT WE'RE HERE WITH FAMILY.

YEAH! LIVING HERE WITH YOU IS GREAT.

A LOT BETTER THAN SHARING THIS SPACE WITH OTHER CATS.

WHEN THEY COME BACK, THEY'RE LAUGHING AND JOKING WITH ONE ANOTHER...JUST LIKE FAMILY. JUST LIKE BROTHERS.

MAYBE BLOOD IS THAT IMPORTANT. MAYBE IT CAN OVERCOME ANYTHING. BUT IF BARLEY IS CHOOSING THEM...

...WHERE DOES THAT LEAVE ME? ...WHAT PLACE DO I HAVE HERE?

HEY, RAVENPAW, CATCH US SOME DINNER, WOULD YOU?

I CAN'T COMPETE WITH THEM. THAT MUCH IS BECOMING OBVIOUS.

EASIER TO JUST...DO AS THEY ASK, I GUESS.

WE'RE STILL GETTING CAUGHT UP WITH BARLEY.

YEAH--IT'S NO PROBLEM.

I'LL GET A MOUSE.

NATURALLY IT DOESN'T TAKE MUCH EFFORT TO CATCH A MEAL. BUT I'M NOT PREPARED FOR WHAT HAPPENS NEXT.

THERE HE IS.

ABOUT TIME.

SO, HEY, WE CAN SLEEP IN YOUR NEST TONIGHT, RIGHT? YOU DON'T MIND, DO YOU?

YEAH--WE'D MAKE OUR OWN, BUT THAT WHOLE CARRYING MOSS UNDER OUR CHINS THING...

WE DON'T HAVE THE HANG OF THAT YET.

PART OF ME WANTS TO CALL THEM LAZY AND WORTHLESS, AND DEMAND THAT THEY GET OUT OF MY NEST.

BUT I DON'T WANT TO CAUSE MORE TROUBLE FOR BARLEY.

SURE... ALL RIGHT.

I CAN ALWAYS MAKE ANOTHER.

I HAVE SORT OF A FAINT HOPE THAT THINGS WILL BE BETTER IN THE MORNING.

GUESS I SHOULD'VE KNOWN BETTER.

HEY, RAVENPAW!

IT'S ALL I CAN DO NOT TO RUSH OVER THERE. STAND BY BARLEY'S SIDE.

BUT THIS IS HIS FIGHT, NOT MINE.

BARLEY NEEDS TO SETTLE THIS ON HIS OWN.

RID HIMSELF OF HIS BROTHERS ONCE AND FOR ALL.

85

ERIN HUNTER

is inspired by a love of cats and a fascination with the ferocity of the natural world. As well as having great respect for nature in all its forms, Erin enjoys creating rich, mythical explanations for animal behavior. She is also the author of the Seekers series.

Visit the Clans online
and play Warriors games at
www.warriorcats.com.

For exclusive information on your favorite authors and artists, visit www.authortracker.com.

DON'T MISS GRAYSTRIPE'S
HARROWING JOURNEY

WARRIORS

THE LOST WARRIOR

WARRIOR'S REFUGE

WARRIOR'S RETURN

Find out what really happened to Graystripe when he
was captured by Twolegs, and follow him and Millie on
their torturous journey through the old forest territory
and Twolegplace to find ThunderClan.

SASHA'S STORY
IS REVEALED IN

WARRIORS

TIGERSTAR AND SASHA

#1: INTO THE WOODS

#2: ESCAPE FROM THE FOREST

#3: RETURN TO THE CLANS

Sasha has everything she wants: kind housefolk who take care of her during the day and the freedom to explore the woods beyond Twolegplace at night. But when Sasha is forced to leave her home, she must forge a solitary new life in the forest. When Sasha meets Tigerstar, leader of ShadowClan, she begins to think that she may be better off joining the ranks of his forest Clan. But Tigerstar has many secrets, and Sasha must decide whether she can trust him.

The #1 national bestselling series, now in manga!

WARRIORS

THE RISE OF SCOURGE

TOKYOPOP®

HARPER COLLINS

ERIN HUNTER

NO WARRIORS MANGA
COLLECTION IS
COMPLETE WITHOUT:

WARRIORS

THE RISE OF SCOURGE

Black-and-white Tiny may be the runt of the litter, but he's also the most curious about what lies beyond the backyard fence. When he crosses paths with some wild cats defending their territory, Tiny is left with scars—and a bitter, deep-seated grudge—that he carries with him back to Twolegplace. As his reputation grows among the strays and loners that live in the dirty brick alleyways, Tiny leaves behind his name, his kittypet past, and everything that was once important to him—except his deadly desire for revenge.

THE #1 NATIONAL BESTSELLING SERIES

WARRIORS

SUPER EDITION

SKYCLAN'S DESTINY

EXCLUSIVE MANGA ADVENTURE INSIDE!

ERIN HUNTER

TURN THE PAGE FOR A SNEAK PEEK AT

WARRIORS

SUPER EDITION

SKYCLAN'S DESTINY

Many moons ago, five warrior Clans shared the forest in peace. But as Twolegs encroached on the cats' territories, the warriors of SkyClan were forced to abandon their home and try to forge a new life far away. Eventually, the Clan disbanded— forgotten by all until Firestar was sent on a quest to reunite its descendants and return SkyClan to its former glory.

Now, with Leafstar in place as leader, SkyClan is thriving. But threats continue to plague the Clan, and as dissent grows from within, Leafstar must face the one question she dreads: Is SkyClan meant to survive?

Floodwater thundered down the gorge, chasing a wall of uprooted trees and bushes as if they were the slenderest twigs. Leafstar stood at the entrance to her den and watched in horror as the current foamed and swirled among the rocks, mounting higher and higher. Rain lashed the surface from bulging black clouds overhead.

Water gurgled into Echosong's den; though the SkyClan leader strained her eyes through the stormy darkness, she couldn't see what had happened to the medicine cat. A cat's shriek cut through the tumult of the water and Leafstar spotted the Clan's two elders struggling frantically as they were swept out of their den. The two old cats flailed on the surface for a heartbeat and then vanished.

Cherrytail and Patchfoot, heading down the trail with fresh-kill in their jaws, halted in astonishment when they saw the flood. They spun around and fled up the cliff, but the water surged after them and carried them yowling along the gorge. Leafstar lost sight of them as a huge tree, its roots high in the air like claws, rolled between her and the drowning warriors.

Great StarClan, help us! Leafstar prayed. *Save my Clan!*

Already the floodwater was lapping at the entrance to the nursery. A kit poked its nose out and vanished back inside with a frightened wail. Leafstar bunched her muscles, ready to leap across the rocks and help, but before she could move, a wave higher than the rest licked around her and caught her up, tossing her into the river alongside the splintered trees.

Leafstar fought and writhed against the smothering water, gasping for breath. She coughed as something brittle jabbed inside her open mouth. She opened her eyes and spat out a frond of dried bracken. Her nest was scattered around her den and there were deep claw marks in the floor where she had struggled with the invisible wave. Flicking off a shred of moss that was clinging to one ear, she sat up, panting.

Thank StarClan, it was only a dream!

The SkyClan leader stayed where she was until her heartbeat slowed and she had stopped trembling. The flood had been so real, washing away her Clanmates in front of her eyes. . . .

Sunlight was slanting through the entrance to her den; with a long sigh of relief, Leafstar tottered to her paws and padded onto the ledge outside. Down below, the river wound peacefully between the steep cliffs that enclosed the gorge. As sunhigh approached, light gleamed on the surface of the water and soaked into Leafstar's brown-and-cream fur; she relaxed her shoulders, enjoying the warmth and the sensation of the gentle breeze that ruffled her pelt.

"It was only a dream," she repeated to herself, pricking her ears at the twittering of birds in the trees at the top of the gorge. "Newleaf is here, and SkyClan has survived."

A warm glow of satisfaction flooded through her as she recalled that only a few short moons ago she had been nothing more than Leaf. She had been a loner, responsible for no cat but herself. Then Firestar had appeared: a leader of a Clan from a distant forest, with an amazing story of a lost Clan who had once lived here in the gorge. Firestar had gathered loners and kittypets to revive SkyClan; most astonishing of all, Leaf had been chosen to lead them.

"I'll never forget the night when the spirits of my ancestors gave me nine lives and made me Leafstar," she murmured. "My whole world changed. I wonder if you still think about us, Firestar," she added. "I hope you know that I've kept the promises I made to you and my Clanmates."

Shrill meows from below brought the she-cat back to the present. The Clan was beginning to gather beside the Rockpile, where the underground river flowed into the sunlight for the first time. Shrewtooth, Sparrowpelt, and Cherrytail were crouched down, eating, not far from the fresh-kill pile. Shrewtooth gulped his mouse down quickly, casting suspicious glances at the two younger warriors. Leafstar remembered how a border patrol had caught the black tom spying on the Clan two moons ago, terrified and half-starving. They had persuaded him to move into the warriors' den, but he was still finding it hard to fit into Clan life.

I'll have to do something to make him understand that he is among friends now, Leafstar decided. *He's more nervous than a cornered mouse.*

The two Clan elders, Lichenfur and Tangle, were sharing tongues on a flat rock warmed by the sun. They looked content; Tangle was a bad-tempered old rogue who stopped in the gorge now and again to eat before going back to his den in the forest, but he seemed to get on fine with Lichenfur, and Leafstar hoped she would convince him to stay permanently in the camp.

Lichenfur had lived alone in the woods farther up the gorge, aware of the new Clan but staying clear of them. She had almost died when she had been caught in a fox trap, until a patrol had found her and brought her back to camp for healing. After that she had been glad to give up the life of a loner. "She has wisdom to teach the Clan," Leafstar mewed softly from the ledge. "Every Clan needs its elders."

The loud squeals she could hear were coming from Bouncepaw, Tinypaw, and Rockpaw, who were chasing one another in a tight circle, their fur bristling with excitement. As Leafstar watched, their mother, Clovertail, padded up to them, her whiskers twitching anxiously. Leafstar couldn't hear what she said, but the apprentices skidded to a halt; Clovertail beckoned Tinypaw with a flick of her tail, and started to give her face a thorough wash. Leafstar purred with amusement as the young white she-cat wriggled under the swipes of her mother's rough tongue, while Clovertail's eyes shone with pride.

Pebbles pattering down beside her startled Leafstar. Looking up, she saw Patchfoot heading down the rocky trail with a squirrel clamped firmly in his jaws. Waspwhisker followed him, with his apprentice, Mintpaw, a paw step behind; they both carried mice. Leafstar gave a little nod of approval as the hunting patrol passed her. Prey was becoming more plentiful with the warmer weather, and the fresh-kill pile was swelling. She pictured Waspwhisker when he had first joined the Clan during the first snowfall of leaf-bare: a lost kittypet wailing with cold and hunger as he blundered along the gorge. Now the gray-and-white tom was one of the most skillful hunters in the Clan, with an apprentice of his own. He even had kits, with another former stray named Fallowfern.

SkyClan is growing.

As their father padded past, Waspwhisker's four kits bounced out of the nursery and scampered behind him, squeaking. Their mother, Fallowfern, emerged more slowly and edged her way down the trail after them; she still wasn't completely comfortable with the sheer cliff face and pointed rocks that surrounded SkyClan's camp.

"Be careful!" she called. "Don't fall!"

The kits had already reached the bottom of the gorge, getting under their father's paws, cuffing one another over the head and rolling over perilously near to the pool. Waspwhisker gently nudged the pale brown tom, Nettlekit, away from the edge.

But as soon as their father turned away to drop his prey

on the fresh-kill pile, Nettlekit's sister, Plumkit, jumped on him. Nettlekit swiped at her, as if he was trying to copy a battle move he'd seen when the apprentices were training. Plumkit rolled over; Nettlekit staggered, lost his balance, and toppled into the river.

Fallowfern let out a wail. "Nettlekit!"

ENTER THE WORLD OF

WARRIORS

Warriors

Sinister perils threaten the four warrior Clans. Into the midst of this turmoil comes Rusty, an ordinary housecat, who may just be the bravest of them all.

Warriors: The New Prophecy

Follow the next generation of heroic cats as they set off on a quest to save the Clans from destruction.

 Also available unabridged from Harper Children's Audio

HARPER

An Imprint of HarperCollinsPublishers

Visit www.warriorcats.com for games, Clan lore, and much more!

Warriors: Power of Three

Firestar's grandchildren begin their training as warrior cats.
Prophecy foretells that they will hold more power than any cats before them.

Grab the first three adventures in the *Warriors: Power of Three Box Set.*

**Don't miss the
stand-alone adventures!**

Warriors: Omen of the Stars

Which ThunderClan apprentice will complete the prophecy that foretells
that three Clanmates hold the future of the Clans in their paws?

Also available
unabridged
from Harper
Children's Audio

HARPER
An Imprint of HarperCollinsPublishers

Visit www.warriorcats.com for games, Clan lore, and much more!